WILLIAM MAYNE

THE·MOUSE AND·THE·EGG

With pictures by
KRYSTYNA TURSKA

 Greenwillow Books, New York

For Julia MacRae

Library of Congress Cataloging in Publication Data
Mayne, William (date)   The mouse and the egg.
Summary: When the speckled hen lays a golden egg,
Grandfather learns the value of her plain brown ones.
[1. Eggs–Fiction]   I. Turska, Krystyna (date)
II. Title. PZ7.M4736Mo [E]   80-15084
ISBN 0-688-80301-6   ISBN 0-688-84301-8 (lib. bdg.)

Once a grandmother   and a grandfather

lived alone in a house high on a hill

with a speckled hen who laid them eggs for tea,

and a long-tailed mouse.

"I wish," said Grandfather one day,
"I wish I did not always have
a brown egg for tea.

First there is the shell,
and then there is the white,
and in the middle is the yellow yolk,
and that is all. I am tired of eggs.
Can we have something better?"

The mouse heard and curled his long tail.

Grandmother heard.
"Oh," she said, "always be thankful.

We have had the eggs boiled,
we have had them fried,
we have had them scrambled,
and we have had them
whisked in milk.
What could be better?"
"I think," said Grandfather,
"we could have
a different sort of egg."
The mouse heard that
and straightened his tail.
Grandmother said,
"Go and ask
the speckled hen."

Grandfather went to ask the speckled hen
in her house across the yard.

She said, "I am sorry I do not please.
You should have spoken sooner.
Come back before tea
and find whatever you find."

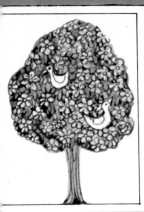

The mouse heard and tied the first knot in his tail.

Grandmother heard.
"It had better be good," she said.
"After all these years
I can only cook eggs."

Then Grandfather had a little sleep.
The mouse watched him and tied the second knot.

Grandmother set the table.

The speckled hen began to sing and call
for Grandfather. She had laid an egg.

He woke and crossed the yard to her
and brought back what he had found.

It was a golden egg.

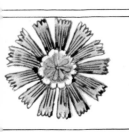
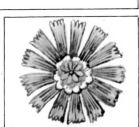
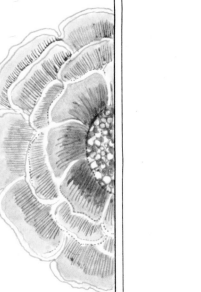

The mouse saw and tied the third knot.
"My goodness, my gracious,"
said Grandmother.   "A golden egg! What next?"
"What more could we want?"
said Grandfather, and he put the egg
on a cushion on a stool.

Grandmother said, "I do not know;
I declare I do not know, I cannot tell,
how to cook a golden egg for tea:
Should I roast or boil?
Should I break the shell?
Should I bake or coddle?
Should I fry in oil?
Or should I put it back again underneath
the speckled hen to see how it will hatch?"

And the egg sat all alone and golden
on the cushion on the stool.
And the mouse undid a knot.

The wind blew
and the door of the little house
banged a little on its latch,
and the golden egg
began to crack.

The mouse undid the second knot,
the fire spluttered in the grate,
the smoke came in the room,
and the golden egg
began to break.

The mouse undid the third knot,
because he knew, he knew.
The soot came down the chimney
and the wind banged in the sky,
and the golden egg fell to dust.

"And that is what we get,"
said Grandmother,
"after all your changes.
That is the only egg
we have, Grandfather.
Are you hungry now?"
"I am," said Grandfather.
"I could eat an egg."
And the mouse
curled his tail round
and went to sleep,
because he knew.

"I am sorry," said Grandfather,
"sorry I spoke against my food.
I shall not do it again."

Outside, the speckled hen
in her little house across the yard
sang a song and called.

Grandmother went out to her
and found what she had to find,
an egg, warm and brown and fresh.
"Thank you, speckled hen,"
she said, and gave her corn
and closed the door.

She went to her own house
and closed the door.

Grandfather and Grandmother had an egg for tea.

"Thank you, Grandmother,"
said Grandfather,
"for cooking my food."
"Thank you, God," said Grandmother,
"for giving it to us every day. Amen."
"Amen," said Grandfather,
"for the shell, for the white, and
for the yellow yolk in the middle."

"Amen," said the mouse.

"Amen," sang the speckled hen.

Printed in Great Britain by Sackville Press Billericay Limited, Essex.